# FORCED INTELLIGENCE

ISBN: 978-0-9839069-5-7

Cover Concept, Artwork and Design: JH Glaze
Text Editing: Susan Grimm
First Printing April 2013
Published by MostCool Media Inc.
"Make it interesting. Make it MostCool."

Proudly printed in the United States of America.

First Edition April 2013

10 9 8 7 6 5 4 3 2 1

*I dedicate this book to my wife Susan, my dogs Harley and Jake, and the other animals that at one time or other have been a part of my life. It is through my interactions with these extraordinary creatures that I have come to the understanding that animals do indeed have feelings and thoughts that we can barely begin to understand.*

*While I have been accused of having a political agenda in this story, I can only say that when writing it, I tried to put myself in the place of the animal and tell their story from their perspective. If that is an agenda, then it is the agenda of the animals in the story, nothing more and I make no apologies for their thoughts and feelings.*

*Forced Intelligence*

*"Intelligence, forced upon an oppressed group without context or experience, is like a bonfire in a paper house."*

J.H. Glaze

# 0735 hrs...

Alex sipped his coffee as he drove along Highway 46. The sun was just above the horizon on this crisp spring morning and the shadows were falling over the road ahead to the rhythm of the trees. He was really enjoying one of his favorite songs coming from the car radio since it was fed through his digital music player on a hand-selected playlist. In fact, he was enjoying it so much that he began singing along, very loudly.

Today was the day he and his team had been working toward these last years. It was a wonder that the music could pull his thoughts away from the coming implications of their successful experiment. He almost didn't notice when the rabbit ran out on the road in front of his new Honda hybrid. His reflexes were a bit slow, but his brakes were brand new, and he managed to step on the pedal and turn the wheel slightly in to avoid the animal.

The car began to skid on the damp pavement and, in what seemed like slow motion, the rabbit disappeared under the front of his car. When the car came to a full stop, his heart was pounding. He looked in the rearview mirror to see if there were any cars behind him, but there was no one else on the road. He put the car in park and stepped out to see what had happened to the rabbit.

As he walked to the front of the car, there was no sign of it. Nothing to the rear but skid marks on the road. He bent down to look under the car. There was the frightened rabbit, hunched down and shivering. "Come on out, buddy. It's okay now. You can go along home," he said, trying to coax the terrified creature out from under the car. The rabbit wasn't moving, obviously feeling safer where it was than with the large animal making the strange noises and reaching for him.

The door-ajar alarm was pinging continuously, and he went back to the open car door and reached into the back seat, retrieving his large old-fashioned golf umbrella. He bent down again and started pushing the rabbit with the wooden handle. Strange that it still would not budge.

After several attempts, Alex decided he didn't have time to keep trying. This was an important day, and he might be late to the lab. As he turned to leave, the rabbit shot out from under the car and ran for the woods, a distance of about twenty-five yards from the road.

Alex stood there a moment watching the little white tail bound away. After hopping off the pavement, the rabbit stopped as if contemplating its close brush with death before disappearing into the woods. Just then, there was a screech, and Alex saw a blur of motion swooping quickly from the right.

The red-tailed hawk was a master hunter. Its deadly claws pierced and lifted its prey from the ground, the rabbit screaming in pain and terror, while Alex watched helplessly.

"After all that, and now you're breakfast? What a bunch of crap! You would have been better off crushed under my tires, Mr. Rabbit. At least it would have been a quick and painless death." Alex envisioned the rabbit being ripped apart as the hawk relished its first meal of the day.

# ...0755 hrs...

Alex reached inside of his satchel and pulled out his security badge as he pulled up to the gate. Since this was a high security lab, there was always at least one if not two armed guards at the entrance at all times. He had been told when he first began working here that the guards had standing orders to shoot to kill, though he wasn't sure whether to believe that or not.

Hawks Mountain was built into the side of a mountain, the previous site of an abandoned mine. This morning there was only one guard at the station and, as Alex approached, he stepped out of the guard shack and held his hand out signaling for Alex to stop. "Good morning, Dr. Connor. I need to see your..." Alex was already holding up his badge. "Okay, have a good day sir."

"You too," Alex replied and pulled through the gate. He turned into the parking lot and found the spot with his name, turned off the ignition and walked toward the entrance. At the first security door, he simply waved his badge over the device and the door opened. He stepped into a hallway and the sliding door closed behind him. The first stage of the entrance procedure was a disinfectant process using UV light and an antibacterial mist that dried almost as quickly as it made contact. It was necessary to retain a constant microbe-free atmosphere within the facility.

Several of the experiments that were conducted in the labs were based on bacterial and viral agents. Alex was subjected to the process even though his research had nothing to do with such biological agents, but was based entirely on forced intelligence and the measurement of intelligence in animals.

The Hawks Mountain facility was federally owned and operated and Alex was well aware that there it was highly likely that the results of his research would one day have military applications. Despite that, he had agreed to work here after all other attempts of obtaining funding in the private sector had been exhausted.

A buzzer sounded the warning that the mist was about to begin. It was only a three-second spray so he always put on his glasses and held his breath for a twenty-second count as soon as the buzzer sounded. That twenty seconds gave him time enough for the fresh air flush that followed before the second buzzer warned of the brilliant flashes of powerful UV light.

When the second warning sounded, he closed his eyes tightly until the flashing stopped and a recorded voice said, *"Please proceed."* A door slid open at the end of the hallway and he walked forward, stopping at the next door and checkpoint. He pressed his right hand against the palm reader and said his name, "Dr. Alex Connor." Another buzzer sounded and the door in front of him slid open.

Inside, sat an armed guard who smiled and greeted him with a hearty, "Good morning, sir." And then, "Dr. Shafer asked that you meet her in her office as soon as you arrive." He nodded and said "Thanks."

# ...0820 hrs...

"So, if we increase the levels of oxygen in the chamber, you think the brain cells will more readily absorb the information?" asked Alex.

"I'm saying that increased oxygen intake contributes greatly to improved alertness and, in some cases learning retention, that's all. Besides we don't have time to implement something like that for the experiment this morning." Donna wrote something on the clipboard she was holding.

"Well," Alex replied, "at least if we want to try implementing that variable, we don't have to put in a requisition for it. We have portable oxygen tanks in the supply room, and all it would take is a simple request form, not that big of a deal."

As he checked the numbers on the power output monitors, he thought back on events, which had brought him to this moment.

He had met Dr. Donna Shafer when he was working in his lab at the UC Berkeley lab two years ago. He had been studying the effects of mild hallucinogens on campus volunteers and the correlation between enhanced visionary experiences and environmental input.

His current project had been a spinoff of that experiment. He had discovered a potential relationship between electromagnetic stimulus of the brain and increased intelligence. This had occurred simply by accident when a student sneaked her cell phone into the lab and received a call at the peak of an interactive exercise designed to measure spatial recognition. Although the call went unanswered, suddenly she was performing much better than she had in previous tests, and the seed for the current project was planted.

Unfortunately for Alex, when he shifted his field of research, he lost his source of funding and was asked to vacate his lab for more "worthy" projects. He interpreted that to mean that the university was reluctant to support a project that could possible render it irrelevant if somehow knowledge could be *transferred* rather than taught.

It was around that same time that he was contacted by the US Air Force. Apparently there was an interest at the Pentagon in the enhancement of the intelligence of pilots and other military personnel. Some believed that it would increase our edge in operations related to strategy, rather than simply "our guns are bigger than your guns."

So after a great deal of emotional wrangling and the gut-wrenching realization that everything he had worked for the past few years would be for nothing without the necessary funding, he made the decision to accept the government's proposal.

Then she broke the silence and brought him back to the present.

"I've been double checking my calculations this morning, Alex, and I think I found an error in our drivers for the damping system. I corrected it but I think, since we have so much riding on this, maybe you should check it before we proceed."

Alex looked at her for a moment, and then replied, "Look, I brought you in on this project because I have total confidence in your work. If you believe you've found an error and corrected it, that's all I need to know. Besides, the damping system is your design; I am more familiar with the other systems. At this late hour, I don't think I could be of much help in checking your work."

Donna smiled, "I just thought I'd ask. I already knew what you'd say."

Alex smiled back "Sure you did. Let's get set up. This is the day we've been working toward, and I want to get it started."

# ...0915 hrs...

Alex and Donna were running equipment checks and testing systems in the control booth, which had been designed to protect the occupants from various types of low-level radiation. It was a square room, twenty by twenty feet, built with a lead barrier embedded in the concrete walls. Cameras had been installed so they could see everything going on in the testing chamber, which was displayed on dual 42-inch monitors hanging from the wall.

Alex could see their lab assistant, Randy, leading Caesar into the brightly lit room. Caesar was a 3-year-old chimpanzee that had been raised by Alex and his team and, in the two and a half years they had worked with him, they had been successful in teaching him basic communication skills and a visual vocabulary of more than 150 words.

When they first started to teach him to communicate with humans, they used an abbreviated form of the standard American Sign Language. The signs were limited to fit the daily routine of a young chimpanzee interacting with his captors. Later, they added computer software designed by a student at MIT and a keyboard for Caesar that used symbols for phrases and concepts. This enabled the chimpanzee to develop a language that was more natural, processing information in pictures and concepts.

This morning Randy asked Caesar to sit in the chair while he went to the small cooler sitting on the table to retrieve a banana smoothie as a reward for Caesars cooperation, for "being a good guy" as Randy put it.

# ... 0920 hrs ...

Alex opened the door and entered the chamber, "Good morning, Caesar. How's my favorite coffee buddy doing this morning?" Caesar looked at Alex and bared his teeth in a chimpanzee smile and signed, "Good."

"Excellent, excellent. Randy, did Caesar have his vitamins last night and this morning?"

"Sure thing, Doc. In fact, the new liquid type must be really good because he kept asking for another cup!"

"I understand. It is fruit flavored, no doubt sweetened too. You know how kids are." He smiled.

"I need you to get him buckled in. We'll be ready to get started in about five minutes." He turned and walked back toward the door. "We'll see you in a few minutes, Caesar. If everything goes as expected, I'll be talking to you!"

As Alex walked out the door, Randy began to fasten the straps designed to make sure that Caesar was secure in the chair during the exposure segment of the experiment. As he bent over to reach the buckle, he accidentally bumped Caesars arm, sending the smoothie sailing across the room. It bounced once off the floor and was stopped by one of the four radiant devices that delivered the energy that would boost the intelligence. That was their theory anyway.

The smoothie splashed across the base of the device. "Damn it, look at the mess! I don't have time to clean that up. After this is over, I'll get a towel and you can help me. Okay, Caesar?"

Caesar looked up at him and signed "Okay, friend."

Donnas' voice came through the audio monitor, "Everything set in there?"

"Sure, I'm heading out. Give me ten seconds." He rubbed Caesar's head saying, "I'll be back in a couple of minutes, buddy." Randy walked out the door, closing it behind him.

# ...0930 hrs...

Alex and Donna were both sitting in front of the computer monitors, checking last minute details. Above them Caesar could be seen in the monitors, looking casually about the room while picking at the hairs on his leg.

"All systems are ready. Do we have power?"

"Twenty seconds to full power"

"Ok, Everything is go."

"In 10, 9, 8, 7, 6, 5, 4, 3, 2, 1"

Alex clicked on the large red 'Engage' button in the middle of the control panel on his screen.

A low hum began to emanate from the equipment.

Alex remembered back to six months ago when it was being decided what type of information they would map through the system into Caesar's brain. Initially the Pentagon had wanted the chimp programmed with details of a military operation that involved infiltration of a building to disable some complex equipment, the outcome of which would justify the funding of the lab.

Instead Alex had pushed back hard, threatening to shut down the project if the first trial was not wholly dedicated to literal intelligence enhancement. After days of communicating back and forth, he had finally persuaded them to agree to implementation using the information stored in an electronic encyclopedia database, which allowed him to move forward with a renewed sense of purpose.

Now here he was, finally fulfilling his vision. He watched the monitor as Caesar began to look confused, baring his teeth and shutting his eyes tightly. Suddenly there was an arc of brilliant energy from the station where Caesar was secured that jumped to the base of the radiant device. As the monitor dimmed, he heard the loud "WHAM" come from the other room.

Everything went black.

"What the hell?" he shouted in the darkness.

"What just happened, Alex?" He could hear Donna bumping into something as she moved across the room toward him.

The emergency lighting kicked in. The usually dormant LED lights cast an eerie backdrop behind the equipment that was now totally dead.

"Oh shit! I think we fried the electrical system," he said looking at the monitors.

Suddenly the emergency alarm kicked on with a blaring intermittent buzzer and a loud female voice saying...

*'Hazardous anomaly detected. Lockdown initiated.'*

"Oh my God, what did we do?"

*'Hazardous anomaly detected. Lockdown initiated.'*

"Donna, grab the mask and a fire extinguisher, I'm going to see..."

*'Hazardous anomaly detected. Lockdown initiated.'*

"...If Caesar is injured..." he said, calling over his shoulder as he ran out the door.

Donna moved toward the emergency cabinet, broke the seal...

*'Hazardous anomaly detected. Lockdown initiated.'*
...and grabbed the hazardous materials mask. She slipped it over her head and...

*'Hazardous anomaly detected. Lockdown initiated.'*
...grabbed a second one before following Alex out the door.

In the short hallway she located the emergency alert kill switch.

*'Hazardous anomaly detected. Lockdown initiated.'*
She opened the cover and hit the red raised button with the palm of her hand.

# ...0945 hrs...

At the Pentagon, the warning was clear. There had been an accident at the Hawks Mountain facility. The lieutenant who had first received the alert put in the call to the officer in charge of the project, a five-star general. The news of the incident had spread quickly and an emergency meeting of all principles of the project had been called in to discuss the situation. The appropriate protocols had been put into place in the event of such an emergency and were now being followed.

\*\*\*

Donna entered the chamber to find Alex pressing two fingers against Caesar's neck. Caesar was slouched forward, either unconscious or expired. "What do you have?" she asked him tentatively, hoping for good news.

"His pulse seems to be strong, I think we need to give it a few minutes. All of the monitoring equipment was fried from the surge."

"What do you think happened?" She looked around the room. "Oh shit! I think I see something!" Donna walked over to one of the three radiant devices and bent over to look for the source of the wisp of smoke coming from the base. "It looks like..." She bent over and touched something with her finger and put it in her mouth. "Oh my God! It is... It's banana smoothie!"

"There must have been a spill in here just before we got started. Where the hell is Randy?" Alex started for the door. "Stay with Caesar and keep an eye out for any odd behavior while I look for Randy. I need to find out what happened here." he said over his shoulder as he was leaving the room.

# ...0950 hrs...

Randy was sitting at his desk, staring through the door. Alex had asked him several times if he was okay, but Randy just sat and stared back at him with saliva oozing from the corner of his partly opened mouth.

"Hey Alex, where was all that noise coming from?" asked a somewhat familiar voice from the corner of the room, startling him.

"What?" he asked, turning to face where JoJo was sitting on the top of his cage.

"You didn't hear the noise? It was really loud, and what is a 'hazardous anomaly' anyway? I think that means something bad, doesn't it?" The African Gray parrot was bobbing as he spoke.

Alex knew that over the course of the past several years, JoJo had managed to learn about a hundred words or so. He even managed to string them into intelligible sentences at times, but this was way beyond anything he had heard from the little guy in the past. He answered the question to see what JoJo might say next.

"Yes JoJo, it means there has been an accident in the facility." He waited for the response, his palms beginning to sweat.

"So... I guess we are in lockdown now, some type of quarantine?"

Alex had no choice to admit the obvious, "Yes, according to protocol, we are most likely in lockdown." He looked back over at Randy who was now playing aimlessly with a stapler from his desk. "I need to go check on Caesar and Dr. Shafer, could you…" he stopped mid-sentence. He was about to ask a parrot to keep an eye on his lab assistant, but that was just ridiculous. Out of the awkward silence JoJo said, "I know there is something wrong with Randy. I do not feel safe in here. Can I come with you?"

"Uh, sure, I guess so." He walked over to the cage and held up his hand for JoJo to step up. Then he moved the bird to his shoulder and headed back toward the lab.

# ...1000 hrs...

At the entrance to the building, the armed guard who had greeted Alex earlier was standing in front of his desk looking at the phone ringing on it. He looked around with a blank stare, as if he didn't know where the sound was coming from or what to do about it. Earlier, when the experiment had begun, he had felt a tingling sensation and then a sharp pain that seemed to be drilling right into his brain, but everything felt peaceful now.

Peaceful, that is, except for the sidearm that had been un-holstered as the pain overcame him. For a moment he'd thought the building was under assault and had drawn the pistol to ward off any possible intruder, but then his mind went blank, and now he was left holding a loaded gun. There was a loud bang and a whirring sound as somehow the trigger went off and the bullet bounced off the concrete floor, ricocheting into the filing cabinet beside the desk.

Lacking any comprehension of what he had just done, but excited by the noise, the guard pulled the trigger again and again emptying the twelve-round clip into various objects in the room: the trash can, a chair in the waiting area, another one in the filing cabinet, and then a direct hit into the control box of the main communication line into the building, severing contact to the outside world.

He smiled a vacant smile as the phone stopped ringing, though he could barely hear anything now over the ringing in his ears.

# ...1003 hrs...

Donna had released the restraints around Caesar's waist and chest without any thought regarding Alex's caution regarding his behavior when he regained consciousness. When Alex returned with JoJo on his shoulder, he quickly re-fastened the restraints. "We don't know how he might react when he wakes up." He looked up at Donna as he fastened the strap on Caesars chest.

"Yes, he may react badly. I've seen him when he is angry, and you wouldn't like him when he's angry," added JoJo tilting his head to get a better look.

Donna looked at Alex, a puzzled expression on her face, and he answered her silent question. "It seems JoJo's vocabulary has been augmented. I haven't had a chance to explore the range of it yet, but I should tell you that Randy seems to have been adversely affected by the surge. He seems to be totally unresponsive at the moment."

"You mean he's dead?" she exclaimed.

"No, nothing like that, though he may be in a trance. He's in his office sitting at his desk and appears to be catatonic. I'm guessing he'll be okay alone for a few minutes though."

Just then, Caesar's chest heaved and he lifted his head. He looked first at Donna, then at Alex, "I... I feel a bit strange." He coughed and continued, "Is there a problem with the lights? It seems a bit dim in here compared to the normal brightness of the room."

Alex began to feel somewhat dizzy, overwhelmed as tears came to his eyes. Not only had the experiment been a success, it was a miracle. Here was a chimpanzee, speaking for the first time in the history of the planet, and he was responsible for making it happen. Donna stepped up and hugged him. "Congratulations, doctor," she said over his shoulder as she squeezed him in her arms. He could feel the dampness of her own tears as she brushed against his cheek, stepping back.

"I understand there is some emotion here, but could someone get me out of these restraints? My back is beginning to ache." Caesar looked from Donna to Alex and smiled.

# ...1015 hrs...

"Come here, Charlie. That's a good boy. Come over here and give me the keys." Nero coaxed the lab assistant, pointing at the locking latch on his cage. The other chimpanzee sat silently hoping for release or they both might be stuck in their cages without any breakfast.

Charlie, who was responsible for feeding the animals and cleaning cages, was standing about three feet from the cage picking his nose intently. It seemed he did not hear the pleas from his captive charge. Then Nero held up his stainless steel water bowl. "Look Charlie, shiny. Shiny, nice bowl, see the funny man?" He tilted the bowl so Charlie could see his reflection in it.

Charlie cocked his head to one side and stepped forward, reaching for the bowl.

"Open the door, Charlie, or just give me the keys and you can have the shiny bowl. You can play with the funny looking man."

"This is hilarious," said one of the other chimps. "Look at the funny man! Bwa-Ha-Ha! I can't believe we have to do this just to get some breakfast."

"Do you mind?" snapped Nero. "I almost had him. Now be quiet and let me work this!"

# ...1033 hrs...

The meeting at the Pentagon was getting underway, and there were no less than three generals seated at the oval table. Folders were being handed out to apprise the attendees of the situation that had occurred at the lab at Hawks Mountain and the protocols that had been established in the event of just such a situation. There was a vacuum of sound except for the rustling of papers as the officers scrutinized the contents of the folders.

"Gentlemen, due to the nature of the research at the facility, we have a contingency plan to either evacuate or eradicate. Our protocol for this situation was developed with intent that the appropriate procedure would be determined based on feedback obtained by contact with the staff. Sergeant?"

"At this time, all communications have been disrupted. Immediately following the incident, we were able to call into the main line. Then we lost our lines and there is now a total blackout. We have no idea what is going on inside of that lab. We are working to reestablish our link but, at the moment, the likelihood of success seems remote."

He continued, "We have a twelve hour window in which to determine the facts and the condition of the personnel. After that, a Halon decontamination followed by a sterilization process will be initiated. The decision you are faced with is whether these procedures will be enforced or other measures will be taken. I do not envy your position. There are currently 75 staff members at Hawks Mountain."

# ...1050 hrs...

All of Caesar's vital signs were good except for his slight headache, and he agreed that he was feeling fine. He and JoJo went along with Alex and Donna to check on Randy who was now dragging his hand along the wall as he went wandering down the hall.

"Randy, it's Caesar, remember? You gave me a banana smoothie a short time ago."

Randy stared at his friend but there was no sign of recognition. Caesar took his hand as the group walked back to the lab. Randy sat in the chair as they used the equipment there to measure his vitals.

"His pulse, temperature, and blood pressure are normal. I just don't understand what's happened to him." Alex hung the stethoscope back on the rolling table where they kept the medical test devices. He continued, "He wasn't in the room with the equipment, and neither was JoJo, but both of them seem to have been affected in obviously dissimilar ways."

"Why do you suppose we weren't affected as well in some way?" Donna flashed the light in Randy's right eye and watched as the pupil contracted.

"I guess the embedded lead in the walls of the observation room protected us from the pulse of energy that was emitted when the system overloaded, but I wouldn't think it would be strong enough to penetrate the other walls and expose Randy. We didn't have the levels calibrated high enough for that."

"So if Randy and JoJo were exposed, with the resulting outcome, what about everyone else here? I mean, I think there are seventy or eighty people in this facility, what about them?"

"What about the other animals?" Caesar asked, then JoJo chimed in, "I bet they want out of their cages. I know I couldn't stand another minute in mine."

# ...1115 hrs...

Nero and the other two chimpanzees stood surrounded by the rest of the lab animals as they faced the dog cages. "I say we don't let them out. They are too unpredictable." The cat licked his paw while he waited for someone else to chime in.

"Oh, I see how it is," said the German shepherd. "The cat is gonna make decisions for you guys now? How convenient, since the cats hate us!"

One of the rats sat up on its hind legs and spoke up. "Cat has a point, but you know, I don't trust the cat all that much either." He looked over at the cat with beady eyes.

Nero countered, "This is a unique situation indeed, but we have been given the opportunity to free ourselves. We must overcome all our differences and work together if we are to accomplish our escape from this hell hole." He turned his head and looked at the other animals who were nodding in agreement. "Besides, if the dogs try hurting anyone, we can handle them. It seems chimpanzees have the strength of five to seven men."

"Oh yeah? Who says you apes are that strong?" the dog sounded upset.

"I'm not exactly sure who said it. I just know that I know it," replied Nero. "Anyway, I will let you two out if you swear to do no harm to the others. Can you agree to that?"

The pit bull glanced over at the shepherd, "Yeah, we can do that, right buddy?" The response was quick, "Sure, right, no problem-o."

Nero moved to the cage and opened it and the dogs strutted out like a couple of tough guys, looking left and right as they passed through the group of animals. "Oh, one more thing..." Nero said as an afterthought, "If you guys so much as ruffle the fur of anyone else, I'll snap your necks."

"Nice way to start a relationship." mumbled the pit bull.

# ...1130 hrs...

The guard at the main entrance was now asleep on the floor. There was still a lingering smell of spent gunpowder in the air and something like the acrid smoke from burned plastic wiring insulation.

Alex surveyed the damage the shooting spree had done to the room, mostly a lot of holes in the walls and furniture. Then he picked up the phone on the desk and listened for a dial tone. He punched the buttons hoping to get a line to the outside, but it was silent. Then he realized why the phone wasn't working.

Beside the desk, below eye level, the last wisps of smoke streamed from the main box for the communication system. Upon closer inspection, he came to see the box been hit by one of the random shots. The circuit board that handled both the phone and Internet lines had a hole clean through it and the hole showed signs of burnout from a short circuit.

"Oh, this is great, just great," he said aloud to himself as he walked to the metal door that was sealing off the entrance. There was a small red light flashing above it and a sign that read:

*This is an automatic security quarantine device. In the event of emergency, only external personnel may open it. To report an anomaly, use the emergency phone located to the right.'*

To his right, he could see the small red box containing the emergency phone. It had a glass cover that read "In Case of Emergency Break Glass." He looked around for something to use to break the glass. The security officer's gun was lying on the floor, it's slide locked back in the empty position. Alex picked it up, and holding the warm barrel in his hand, he smashed the glass with the grip of the weapon.

He tossed the gun to the side and reached in to grab the handset located inside the red box. Alex put it to his ear, and pressed the call button. Nothing. No dial tone, no answer, and no sound at all. Obviously this phone was connected to the main box.

"Lovely. What a good emergency plan that ties all of the lines into one box." And he headed down the hall back to the lab.

# ... 1 1 45 hrs ...

"Gentlemen, I have spoken to the President and he has decided to allow at least ten more hours for personnel inside of Hawk's Mountain, if they are in fact alive and able, to repair their communication systems." The General nodded to his assistant who dimmed the lights and the giant monitor on the wall flashed to life.

The image on the wall was a photo of the exterior of the facility. He held up his laser pointer, "We have mobilized two tactical squads, who are positioned here and here. The guards who were on duty at the time of the incident have been removed from their posts. Due to the sensitive nature of the work conducted inside the laboratories, we cannot risk outside infection caused by a guard who may not be willing to shoot on sight if the situation requires it. This is standard procedure."

He continued, "In 1989, there was a similar incident in a facility located in Kentucky. There was a containment accident, which caused the release of a viral substance. All of the staff was infected and many died in the first two hours. Those who did not perish were reduced to raving maniacs who proceeded to slaughter one another. When the exit was compromised, the guards on duty hesitated to fire on the people they had come to know on a day-to-day basis. Unfortunately, they were torn to pieces as they tried to reason with the compromised staff members."

All eyes followed the general as he walked toward the monitor and nodded at his assistant for the next slide. "These photos were taken before the sterilization of the area." The scene on the monitor was total carnage. There were three distinct torsos lying in a triangular pattern on the ground. Two were headless, the other one lay with head intact but a large part of the stomach had been ripped out. Though there were only three bodies in the shot, there were about thirteen limbs, shredded arms and legs, strewn about.

"Gentlemen, you may notice a disproportion of body parts lying in the photo. It is reported that not only did the infected overrun the guards, some of them literally tore each other apart as they ran for the tree line."

The next slide showed charred terrain, trees burned to the roots, nothing but rocks and the ground still intact. "A napalm strike was called in and the damage to the forest was reported as a forest fire. One hundred and two were lost that day, including fifteen of my best soldiers. When the infection got out, we had no choice but to destroy anyone and everyone in the area who had been exposed. The cameraman who shot the previous photo gave his own life to record the incident, and the photo you saw was the *least* of the gore that was recorded."

He nodded again to his assistant and the screen faded as the lights came back up in the room. "You see, gentlemen, we can't risk another situation like this. There are seventy-five people in that facility; all of them just like you and me. People who understood that a day like today could possibly come, but were willing to make the ultimate sacrifice for their country."

He paused. "God willing, there was an error in the system, or perhaps a minor accident that tripped the emergency lockdown. But if in fact we have another Kentucky on our hands, we must not hesitate to do our jobs to protect the innocent civilians living in the area and the soldiers who are counting on us to make the right decision."

# ...1200 hrs...

Alex walked into the lab where Donna, Randy and Caesar were waiting. Standing in front of Randy, Caesar was trying everything he could think of to get a response and getting frustrated that Randy was obviously catatonic.

"What did you find, Alex?" Donna could see the look of concern on his face.

"The phones are out, all of them. The guard at the front desk is in no better condition than Randy, but he obviously had the wherewithal to pull the trigger on his sidearm and shoot up the office." He sighed heavily," and, in the process, he took out the main communications board. I tried the emergency phone but it's dead too."

"So what do we do now, Alex?" asked Caesar stepping away from Randy.

"Well, I already tried my cell. I never have been able to get a signal inside of this building, so we have to either find a way to get the doors open, or wait for the feds to come in after us..." He stopped.

"What is it, Alex?" Donna reached out and touched his arm. She'd never known Alex to be so hesitant.

"This is a military facility, and there are other experiments being conducted here besides ours. I'm sure you are aware of that." He looked down at the floor.

Donna started, "Yes, I am aware that there is other work being done here, mostly research on the effects of anti-personnel equipment and..."

Alex cut her off. "And I'm concerned that we are unable to contact anyone on the outside. Since we're in an

"Anomaly" lockdown, the feds may decide to implement sterilization protocols. They may decide to eliminate everything inside this mountain."

"You mean kill us all? But I thought our contract stated that no biological agents were being developed here?" Donna looked at him in shock.

"It is a government facility after all, isn't it?" asked Caesar. "Do you think they were actually telling you the truth?"

# ... 1 2 1 4 hrs ...

"How many more are there?" asked Nero as the cats drove two lab workers ahead of them, biting and scratching at their ankles.

"How would we know? We have only seen Charlie and a couple of other people since we got here. They didn't exactly let us roam the halls," replied the male orange tabby.

"I remember when I could roam free, when I lived with old lady Fiona." The female Siamese mix added, "I had the run of the house and did anything I wanted. That is, until the morning I went to wake her. I stood on her chest as usual, but she never opened her eyes again. That was so sad. She smelled pretty bad by the time her selfish daughter finally came to check on her and I was so hungry by then, I almost took a bite out of her."

"Listen, cat! We're not here to reminisce about the past. These people were going to do some bad things to you, just like they did to your friend. You would have died the same way and ended up in the incinerator with him. We need to get all of the humans gathered up and locked away so they can't harm us anymore!" Nero was clearly agitated as he looked down the hall for the next group.

# ...1230 hrs...

"Do you think there are others like us, who weren't affected?" Donna held Caesar's hand as she followed Alex slowly down the hall.

"I can't be sure. I mean, I don't think there were any other rooms equipped with the lead shielding. We were the only ones working with low level radiation, as far as I know."

As they passed each room, Alex looked through the glass into the rooms or opened the office doors to check for other people who might be in the same condition as Randy. Thus far they had found three, two men and a woman, all wearing white lab coats.

The woman had a stream of vomit down the front of her and it looked like she had tried to eat something from the printer since her mouth had toner stains all around it. They had found her standing at her desk; banging her paperweight on a silver framed picture of some man they guessed might be her husband. The men were just wandering aimlessly in the halls.

As they encountered each person, Caesar would take them by the hand and lead them to the cafeteria. There he would sit them at a table and give them a bag of chips or a bagel from the breakfast buffet to keep them occupied. The trio neared an intersection of hallways when they heard voices coming from around the corner.

"Just because you are larger than me doesn't give you the right to tell me what to do," the impish voice complained.

They rounded the corner and realized who was having the disagreement.

"Yeah" said the pit bull, glaring at the rat, "but if you don't do it, I'll crush your ass with my great and powerful jaws." Just then he noticed the humans.

"Oh my God!" said Donna holding her hand to her mouth, "It's affected all of the animals!"

"Hey, what are you two doing down there?" Alex asked walking toward the duo.

The dog growled and bared his teeth, but Alex could have sworn the dog was mumbling '*motherfucker*' as he got nearer.

# ...1247 hrs...

"Is that all of them?" Nero asked as he stood outside the door of the cage room where most of the animals were kept.

"How would we know? I don't think any of us has ever counted them." The rabbit held it's front feet up and out as if to imitate a shrug.

"I saw a few in some of the rooms who were dead. It appears the experiments they were working on got the best of them. That should teach them to play with dangerous toys!" It was Waldo, the orangutan who hadn't been seen in a while. He was recovering from an experiment that disrupted the cells in his nervous system. He had nearly died as a result. Nero was surprised that he could still walk, though he did so with a terrible limp.

"Are you sure they were dead? We don't need any surprises right now, especially since our ultimate goal is to get out of this place, not to babysit a bunch of no-brain humans!" Nero was scowling at the thought of it.

"I am not about to go into even one of those rooms to check. There was blood in some and vomit in others. Besides, the doors had security locks on them, and I couldn't open them without breaking them down," Waldo replied rubbing his sore leg.

"I understand. They got what they deserved, but it might not have been as slow and painful as it could have been. Let's finish up, then we can decide how to dispose of this trash." Nero waved his arm at the room containing about forty doctors, technicians, lab assistants and Charlie.

# ...1315 hrs...

The meeting at the Pentagon had broken up and would not reconvene unless the conditions at Hawk's Mountain changed significantly, though no one expected it. Communications were still down and if anyone capable of fixing the system were still alive, they should have made contact by now. There were many personnel in the facility with the skills to repair such a unit, and they had a large supply of spare electronics they could cannibalize to get the necessary parts.

The general sat as his desk with his face resting in his hands, and rubbed his eyes to try to reduce the pain from the headache he had been dealing with all morning. He couldn't get the images of the Kentucky incident out of his head. He had been sent to deal with the crisis firsthand when he was just a grunt, going into the hellish scene left after the sterilization more than twenty years ago.

Tears welled in his eyes as he thought about the families that would have to be contacted – and lied to, to cover up all of this. The wives, the husbands, and children. Oh God, the poor children.

# ... 1 3 3 0 hrs ...

JoJo was resting on the back of a chair in the cafeteria while Alex, Donna and Caesar guided the nine workers down the halls from the room where the dog had been holding them at bay. He looked around the room, stretching his neck. "Anyone in here up for some snappy conversation?"

Several heads turned to look at the talking parrot but most of them paid no attention as they picked at the food that they had been given. The group of humans came shuffling in followed by their guides. "These people are a riot," complained JoJo. "I was about to set somebody on fire to see if I could get a reaction." Alex looked at him sternly, and the bird added, "Just joking."

"Not very funny, JoJo," added Donna. "How would you feel if it was you who had lost any awareness of what was happening around you?"

"I guess that would be bad," the bird responded looking at the floor.

"We have more important things to worry about, guys. We need to find the others. The rat told us that Nero and the other animals were rounding them up. They might even kill some of the doctors out of revenge," Alex said as he pulled out a chair and helped one of the young women to sit down. "Any ideas?"

"It would seem natural for the others to put the humans in the cage room, especially if they are talking about revenge. What better revenge than to let them feel what it is like to live in a cage?" Caesar offered.

"It must be terrible, Caesar. I hope you understand that sometimes animals are kept in cages for their own protection, so they won't get hurt by the other animals?" Donna was trying to defuse a difficult conversation before it went too far but, as far as Caesar was concerned, she was actually stirring it up.

"Well, doctor, please explain how someone like me should worry about being harmed by one of the other animals, considering that I'm probably one of the most well-equipped to defend myself?" Caesar clearly was becoming upset, and Alex needed to interrupt this somehow.

"Caesar, would you agree that the safety of everyone in this building, including the animals, is the most important thing for us to focus on right now? Can we set this argument aside until we have made sure everyone is taken care of?"

"I guess you are right, doctor, we will finish this later." He looked at Donna with a furrowed brow, and walked over to the counter to get some bagels for the new arrivals.

# ...1405 hrs...

Now that he was satisfied that most of the humans had been rounded up and locked in the cage room, Nero led the animals down the halls toward the cafeteria to confront the only two doctors who were reported to be in their normal state.

"Remember, they have Caesar with them, and we do not know his state of mind. So far it appears that he has chosen to remain on the side of the humans since he has been helping them all day." Nero spoke as he walked, "We must convince him to help us put those two in the cage room so we can make our escape. I don't want any violence... and that goes for you dogs, too!"

"But you have seen the violence they have committed against us, and you know about how they treat each other, killing themselves with crime, drugs, and war! They kill without conscience or regard. Why should we treat them with anything but violence now that we have the chance to do so before we escape?" Waldo scratched his head as he awaited the reply.

"We cannot be sure of Caesar. He could kill many of us before we could subdue him. We must think and be cautious. Now everyone, be silent, we are getting close. Rat, run ahead and survey the situation then report back. We'll wait here."

Five rats replied simultaneously, "Me?"

Nero pointed at the one standing at the front of the group. "You go."

# ...1408 hrs...

The animals watched as the rat scurried down the hall and returned to report what he had seen. There was a rustle and a murmur as he came near. The animals were growing restless.

Stopping before Nero, the rat spoke. "There are many of them, but only two are able to speak. All of the others are like the ones we put in the cage room."

"And Caesar, is he helping them, or holding them hostage?" asked Nero.

"They were planning what to do next, what to do about... us." The rat's report abruptly came to an end, and he took his place with the other rats.

"I see, we must be extra cautious, we must..." he hesitated.

"Convince him?" asked a rabbit.

"Yes, convince him to see things our way, to our advantage," finished Nero.

Suddenly, from around a corner, Caesar stepped up to the group, "Nero, old friend!" He smiled and went on, "Did you really send a rat scout to see what we were up to?"

"Well, certainly! A single rat scout is much better at covert ops than a rat pack!" He smiled back.

# ...1417 hrs...

The two groups stood across from each other in the cafeteria. The staff, who were quietly sitting at the tables, seemed oblivious to what was happening in the room around them. After a few moments of silence, Nero spoke. "I understand your situation, doctor, but you and your fellow humans will have to come with us."

"I told you, we are all in danger here. It makes no sense to lock us up when we all need to get out of this facility before steps are taken to neutralize the whole place." Alex pleaded, "If we don't work together, we may all die in here."

"They are just saying that to try to save their miserable hides!" A cat yelled from the back of the group and others began chiming in.

"I think we should do to them what they did to us!"

"Yeah, put them in the *pain* room, and make them suffer like I did!"

"Suffering is not good enough! Remember how many of us they have killed?"

Caesar held his hand out, "Stop, all of you. We need to come to determine a course of action here. We need to be rational."

"Rational?" A small voice came from within the crowd and a rat stepped slowly forward, a large tumor dragged from its side onto the floor. "Look at me! Look at what they have done to me! They poked and prodded and injected me with things that made me howl in agony. And they slaughtered my mate. I know they have done as much to others here in this room. I say we exterminate them!"

Several of the animals repeated, "Yeah, exterminate them!"

"Put them down just like they did the dogs at the pound they stole me from!" the German shepherd added.

"Kill them!" The animals were all calling out various forms of execution when Caesar yelled, "Enough!" and the grumbling faded to silence.

Alex spoke next, "Look, I understand that most of you have suffered terrible things in this place, and I do not blame you for wanting revenge, but I know that all of you know that it's wrong to summarily execute all the people here. We at least deserve to have a hearing, or a trial to let us tell out side of the story."

"He's right, Nero. Justice demands that they be heard," Caesar added, but Nero stood silent.

"This will take too long. There are many people here, and they can hardly walk let alone present a defense. There are a few who have done things so horrible, *they* should be put down immediately." The rabbit cocked its ears waiting for a response from the group.

"I hear they do that with dogs who bite people," yelled out one of the cats.

"No, Caesar is right. If we do not allow at least a hearing, we are as bad as they are. We will give them a brief time to talk over their defense, hear them out and then if we remain unconvinced, we will lock them in a room and set fire to the building before we leave." Nero looked at the animals. Waldo was nodding, but many others appeared aggravated.

"I can agree to that. Doctors, can you agree?" said Caesar.

"Do we have a choice?" asked Donna.

"Yes," said Nero, "we can end this right now, right here if you choose. We can make it quick, but I cannot promise it would be painless."

Alex nodded, "Then we choose the hearing."

"Damn!" came the voice of one of the rats hidden in the group.

# ... 1 500 hrs ...

The two special tactical squads were now in place. Soldiers in white full-coverage HAZMAT suits carrying automatic weapons had covered every possible exit. A decontamination unit had been brought in and the doctors who were assigned to this unit were being briefed on worst-case scenario procedures.

Everyone knew the risk involved if just one infected human escaped, and no one was willing to take the chance of allowing it to happen. Not only was this group of soldiers on high alert, they were operating on high anxiety.

# ...1502 hrs...

The Generals aide knocked on the door and he responded, "Come in."

"General, sir, the Vice President is on 1."

"Thank you," he replied as he picked up the phone. "Good afternoon, Mr. Vice President, what can I do for you this afternoon?"

"General, we are all aware of the situation at Hawk's Mountain, and there is concern regarding the deadline we initially set for 22:00 hours."

"Yes sir. What are my orders, sir?"

"The President has requested that the deadline be moved to 18:00 hours so that it is still daylight and you have about an hour and a half before sunset. This will ensure that we do not repeat the 1989 disaster… will eliminate the possibility of someone escaping into the surrounding forest."

The general allowed a sigh to escape.

"Did you say something, General?"

"No sir. We will take the appropriate action at 18:00 hours exactly and…"

"Report to me when the deadline has been updated, please."

"Yes sir, will do, sir." There was a click on the other end, and the general eased the handset back into its cradle and looked at his watch. Just past 15:00 hours. Less than three hours to go.

He bowed his head and began to pray…

# ...1600 hrs...

Donna and Alex sat quietly as the testimony from the animal witnesses continued.

For the past hour and a half they had been hearing what could only be described as horror stories that rivaled the stories that had been told by the Holocaust survivors. Rabbits, rats, mice, cats, dogs and primates told of being overdosed with toxic chemicals, injected with viruses, exposed to impacting anti-personnel devices, operated on and having vital organs removed, and sometimes being dissected while fully conscious. Many of their friends had suffered this and more, and were ultimately killed and incinerated like so much garbage.

Donna had streaks down her cheeks from her running mascara as the tears flowed during the testimony. Alex continually wiped away the tears forming in his eyes to keep his own vision from being blurred. The other humans in the room were oblivious to the proceedings and only occasionally made a moaning sound that interrupted the testimony.

It seemed as if the last animal, a rabbit, was about to speak as it stepped forward and began in a quiet voice, "You can see the shaved patch on my back and the large sores that I have acquired in the last few days due to the application of God knows what. But that is not what I want to talk about."

He looked around the room at the humans seated at the tables. "There is a greater crisis outside of these walls. It is larger than the issue at hand. There is the destruction of our planet, our habitat, by the humans." There was nodding in agreement from some of the other animals.

Alex gasped at this statement. *How did these animals know about environmental issues? They had never seen a news broadcast, read a newspaper or had any access to the Internet. If the rabbit brings up global warming, a phenomenon yet to be agreed upon, I am going to shit.* He thought to himself.

The rabbit continued, "Your own scientific community has been studying man made climate change and many agree that if nothing is done about pollutants being spewed into our environment, this planet will soon be underwater. I remember a great deal of discussion of Global Warming"

Alex's spirit sunk to a new low. He could defend himself against the accusations of atrocities that took place inside of the facility. He had never done anything to harm the animals he worked with. But the damage done to the environment by the entire human race would be impossible to explain.

Finally the rabbit finished his testimony, "So I say these humans are a large part of the problem, not only for what they have done to us, but for what they have done to our entire planet. I say put them down, they do not deserve another chance."

# ...1659 hrs...

Two tactical squads were on last minute preparation alert. Snipers were positioned with clear visibility at all possible points of exit from the facility. One of the commanders was walking the perimeter making a last minute check when a large black SUV pulled up and two men jumped from it.

"Sir, we've brought the hellfire as ordered. When we get the units unloaded, where do you want them to be deployed?" inquired the larger of the two men.

"We want 'em right at the first line. We can't take a chance that any infected break the perimeter. I need that assembled and ready to go in five. You got it, soldier?"

"Yes sir, commander sir!"

# ... 1 7 1 5 hrs ...

It was time for Alex to speak and he had been thinking about what to say as the charges piled up against him and his co-workers. Thoughts raced through his mind and he wanted to be very careful about what he might say. So he began.

"Most of what all of you say is entirely true and I will not waste our time here to defend it, because outside of this facility there are other humans, military types, who are right now deciding our fate. Each moment we waste could result in the death of every one here."

He continued, "Indeed, the experiments conducted in these labs were heinous and caused many of you harm, but *we* humans had no way of knowing how horrible things were for some of you. Our experiments were isolated, and none of the people here knew what the others were doing. From what you have said, some of your animals were able to exact revenge on their tormentors after the incident, and I do not blame any of them. Nor would I condemn them for doing just as humans and observing the right to self defense."

He paused for a second and went on, "But right now outside of this facility they are waiting to hear from us. All communications have been severed and, for them, it appears that the accident in this building might compromise the safety of the people outside of this building. They most likely fear that a virus may have been released and unless we are able to reassure them that indeed that was not the case, they will initiate protocols that will likely kill everything and everyone in the building."

Now he brought out his strongest argument. "So I propose that all of you try to understand this, if we do not work together to get out of this building, we will all surely die. Once we have reached the outside, I will represent your case to the other humans and negotiate your passage from this area."

The animals stared at Alex in stunned silence.

Nero spoke, "So you are saying that if we do not work together, there are humans outside who will kill all of us, including their own kind?"

"He's lying!" The cries came from the group. "I don't believe him!" "He's just trying to save his own ass!" "I say kill all of them now and burn the building down!"

"Quiet!" shouted Nero.

"Doctor, I have known you for some time and believe you are a man of your word. If you tell me there is no other way than to work together, I must believe it. But you said earlier the building is sealed. How can we even get out of here?" Caesar seemed to be trying to help.

"So are you willing to do this my way?" Alex asked.

"We do it, or we *all* die?" Nero asked again.

"Exactly." Alex nodded.

"Then let's get started immediately. Where is the way out?" Nero looked around at the three doorways in the room.

# ... 1740 hrs...

The general dialed the phone number, which was a direct line to the Vice President. The phone rang once, twice... "Talk to me."

"Yes sir, I am calling about the situation at Hawk's Mountain, sir. Our deadline of 18:00 hours is nearly upon us and I regret to inform you that we have had no word from the inside of the facility and there has been no activity reported. Shall we continue as planned, sir?"

""Yes, I hope your men are ready. Let's put this to bed, General." There was a click on the other end of the line.

# ... 1744 hrs ...

Alex, Donna, and all of the animals were crowded into the entryway area of the facility. Alex, Caesar, and Nero were studying the heavy security door that had slid into place when the alert had sounded.

"How are we going to get that door open? It looks very heavy." Caesar scratched his head.

"We can't get it open using any type of keypad because it is controlled from the outside. I think we will have to try to pry it open." Alex put his hand on the door.

"We are stronger than you. With Caesar, Waldo and me, we may be able to do it," replied Nero.

"Okay then. There are two doors that have to be opened, the emergency door and the regular security door. I believe the regular door slides from left to right, so I'm guessing this one does also. If we can open this door, we still have to get the other one open. Nero, you and Waldo take this door. Caesar, after they get this one opened, you pull the other one back at least far enough for Donna and I to get through. Then we will go out first and explain the situation to the military personnel outside."

"Right," Caesar agreed.

Nero and Waldo stepped up and grabbed the cross braces on the heavy door and began to pull. Alex winced as, for the first time, he saw the shaved area on Waldo's back and the horrible sores that must have been caused by one of the experiments carried out on him. Nero's muscles flexed and the two of them made grunting noises as they strained to pull the massive door open.

After about a minute, Nero roared and the door began to slide open slowly. Then he shrieked as blood began to spurt against the door from one of his paws. He reflexively let go of the door and it slid shut. Alex rushed forward and grabbed the injured paw. The blood sprayed all over his white lab coat and into his face. "Give me a towel or something! Hurry!"

Donna quickly removed her lab coat and stepped up to help. She wrapped it around the bleeding paw and using the sleeves as a kind of tourniquet, pulling them tight and tying them together.

Nero had a crazed look in his eyes, and Alex was afraid he might pass out. Bravely, Nero gathered himself and said, "Let's get this done." He stepped back to the door. Caesar put his hand on his shoulder and said, "Let me get this. You should be able to handle the other door."

Waldo made eye contact with Caesar as he grabbed the door and began pulling at it. He fell in with him grunting and pulling as hard as he could. The door slid open about six inches before they had to take a break, but this time it did not slide shut when they released it.

# ... 1 756 hrs ...

The squad commander spoke into his communicator. "Gentlemen, we are four minutes from release. If anything is going to happen, it will be in the next few minutes. Do not relax your positions. We must wait for the all clear."

The soldiers who had lowered their weapons to the 'at ease' position now raised them and sighted on the doorway leading out of the facility. The two soldiers who had been assigned to the hellfire flamethrowers, stood ready, a small flame coming from the barrel of their weapons.

# ... 1 7 5 8 hrs ...

Waldo and Caesar gave one last pull on the door and it was open far enough for Nero to step inside of the opening. They collapsed to the floor, entirely spent of any strength they had left.

Now it was up to Nero, with his injured hand he must open the final door that blocked their exit into the hallway. He stepped forward and began to pull the door to the side, blood dripping from the lab coat wrapped around his hand. He held on to the door and pulled with all of his might. Finally, it began to slide, then slipped from his hands and slammed back shut.

# ... 1759 hrs ...

Nero grabbed the door again with both hands and pulled hard. It slid open as before, but now he held on. He looked back at Alex and commanded, "Go, make the arrangements!"

Alex stepped through the door, but as Donna tried to follow him, Nero stood in the doorway blocking her exit.

"Alex!" she yelled past Nero as he disappeared down the hall.

He turned to look, and with Nero glaring at him, he said, "What the hell?"

Nero smiled and said "Insurance! Now go!"

Alex ran to the last door and swiped his passcard on the sensor, but the door did not open. "I need help with this one!" he yelled down the hall.

Nero looked at Caesar. "You need to get that door. I'll hold this one."

As Nero shifted to one side, Caesar ran through the doorway and down the hall. As he got to the end of the hall, he slid up to the door and pulled with every bit of strength he had left.

# ...1800 hrs...

In the room where Donna, Nero and the other animals were, the Halon gas nozzles hissed to life. "Oh shit, Halon!" screamed Donna; trying to cover her mouth and nose with the sweater she was wearing.

Nero turned to look and lost his grip on the door. As it slammed shut, it spun him around and back into the room. He fell, his bloody arm still in the doorway, and the door slammed on his arm severing it just below the elbow. He roared from the pain and, as he lost consciousness, he caught a glimpse of Donna and the other animals slumping and falling to the floor as the gas overcame them.

At the last exit door, Alex and Caesar were oblivious to what was happening behind them. Caesar pulled as hard as he could and the door slid open. "Go!" he yelled at Alex, and Alex ran through the door into the blaze of light from the setting sun.

He tried to cover his eyes from the glare with his arms and he realized just then he was still wearing the bloody lab coat. He was in the open now and he flailed his arms as he tried to get the lab coat off.

"There's one over there!" One of the soldiers yelled.

The commander looked up from the floor plan he was studying and put his binoculars to his face. He saw Alex flailing there with his bloody lab coat. "Oh my God, he's infected." He yelled into his communicator, "Put him down!"

Alex looked up as the soldiers opened fire. He opened his mouth to scream *Wait!* but the words never escaped his lips as the soldiers' bullets ripped him to pieces. One of the soldiers with a flamethrower stepped from the line and fired on what was left of Alex, training the flame on him until he was left in a sizzling pile in the center of the courtyard.

Inside the entry hall, Caesar witnessed Alex's fate. He let the door slide shut when he saw his friend cut down mercilessly by the soldier's gunfire. Behind him, down the hall, Nero's, severed arm lay on the floor. Everyone on the other side of that door was surely gone now. The room and building filled with deadly Halon gas. There was literally nowhere for him to escape. He was trapped.

As he sat waiting for whatever would come next, he thought about all that had happened to them that day, and the new found intelligence he possessed. The knowledge that had been passed to him through the experiment only hours ago seemed so pointless now when there was no possibility of ever leaving this place.

Tears ran down his cheeks, and he thought about Alex as he stared at the door and heard the soldiers outside trying to open it. After a few seconds, the door slid open, and he said the only thing he could think of at this last moment in his short life. It was the first word he had learned to sign when he was a much younger chimp.

Now he could say the word out loud. "Papa," and he closed his eyes.

■ ■ ■

Also Available From J.H. Glaze:

The Paranormal Adventures of John Hazard:

The Spirit Box – Book I

NorthWest – Book II

Send No Angel – Book III

Ghost Wars – Book IV (coming soon)

The Life We Dream – Novella

Forced Intelligence – Novella

The Horror Challenge Volumes I, II, III

RUNE – A Serial Novel

Books by JH Glaze Can Be Found On Most Book Retail Web Sites In eBook or Paperback Editions.

Follow JH Glaze on Facebook
Twitter: @themostcoolone
Website www.JHGlaze.com
Goodreads.com

*Thank You For Reading!*

www.ingramcontent.com/pod-product-compliance
Lightning Source LLC
Chambersburg PA
CBHW020559130626
46552CB00007B/2951